For Nana

(Centenarian & pigeon fancier)

A TEMPLAR BOOK

First published in the UK in 2018 by Templar Publishing,
an imprint of Kings Road Publishing, part of the Bonnier Publishing Group,
The Plaza, 535 King's Road, London, SW10 0SZ
www.bonnierpublishing.com

ISBN 978-1-78370-001-1 (Hardback)
ISBN 978-1-78370-062-2 (Paperback)

Designed by Genevieve Webster
Edited by Alison Ritchie

Printed in China

The Trussell Trust runs a network of over 425 foodbanks, giving emergency food
and support to over 550,000 people in crisis across the UK every year.

To donate money to the charity:
call **01722 580178** or visit **www.trusselltrust.org/get-involved/ways-to-give**

THE LAST CHIP

The Story of a Very Hungry Pigeon

DUNCAN BEEDIE

templar
books

Life on the streets was tough for Percy the pigeon.
He was ALWAYS hungry.

Every morning he trotted to the railway station and waited patiently
for the first train to arrive. If he was lucky, he might catch a crumb or two
as the commuters hurried on their way to work.

The only trouble was . . .
today Percy wasn't alone.

A gang of greedy pigeons had the same idea.
Percy was so small that when the crumbs came tumbling down,
he was buffeted out of the way.

"SHOVE OFF – that's MINE!" snarled a gruff pigeon
with stumpy toes, as he swallowed the last scrap of food.

Percy's tummy rumbled.

What am I going to eat now? he thought . . .

. . . I know!

It was a very long way to fly, but Percy had heard that at the park,
people actually threw seed in the pond for birds to eat!

So, flapping his little wings as fast as he could,
Percy fluttered high above the city rooftops.

When Percy finally landed in the park he was
hungrier than ever. The only trouble was . . .

. . . he wasn't alone. The pond was full of
greedy ducks gobbling up all the seeds.
But Percy bravely waded in anyway.

"QUAAAAACCCKK! Get out of our pond, you SCOUNDREL!"
bawled the ducks, thrashing at him with their wings.

Percy scrambled back to the bank, and shook the water
from his feathers.

"I'm so hungry!" he gasped. "I **must** find something to eat."
Then he had an idea. He had heard that there were lots of
tasty scraps to be had at the seaside.

So Percy flapped his little wings faster than ever,
and before long, he was flying over a beautiful sandy beach.

Percy was so excited, he forgot to look where he was going.

Before he knew it, he crash-landed and went whooshing and whirling . . .

down to the very bottom of a helter skelter.

Percy couldn't believe it – there, right in front
of his beak, was a scrumptious piece of fish.

"At LAST!" he cried, jittery with delight.

The only trouble was . . .

. . . Percy wasn't alone.
"AAARRRRRRR!" roared a giant seagull. "THERE BE NO PICKINGS
FOR LAND-LUBBIN' VERMIN LIKE THEE!"

Percy's little legs trembled as the terrifying pirate gull
stomped on the piece of fish.

Then he grabbed Percy, slam-dunked him into the
nearest rubbish bin and scoffed the whole lot for himself.

"It's no good," sobbed Percy
as he peeked out from the bin.
"I'll never get **anything** to eat."

And he set off on the
long journey back home.

By now, Percy was so weak with hunger
he could scarcely manage to
flap his little wings at all.
And soon he was swerving and dipping
above the city skyline, before
plummeting to the streets below.

He landed on the pavement with a
THWUMP!

Ignored by the commuters rushing home for their dinners,
Percy prepared himself for another hungry night ahead.

Then he heard a gentle voice . . .

"Excuse me, you look hungry too. Would you like my last chip?"
"For ME?" cried Percy. "Thank you!"

Quivering with excitement, Percy pecked away,
savouring every delicious beakful.

A tingling warmth spread through his body.

Tired and very full, Percy nestled up
next to his new friend.

And for once, the streets didn't feel quite so tough.

THE END

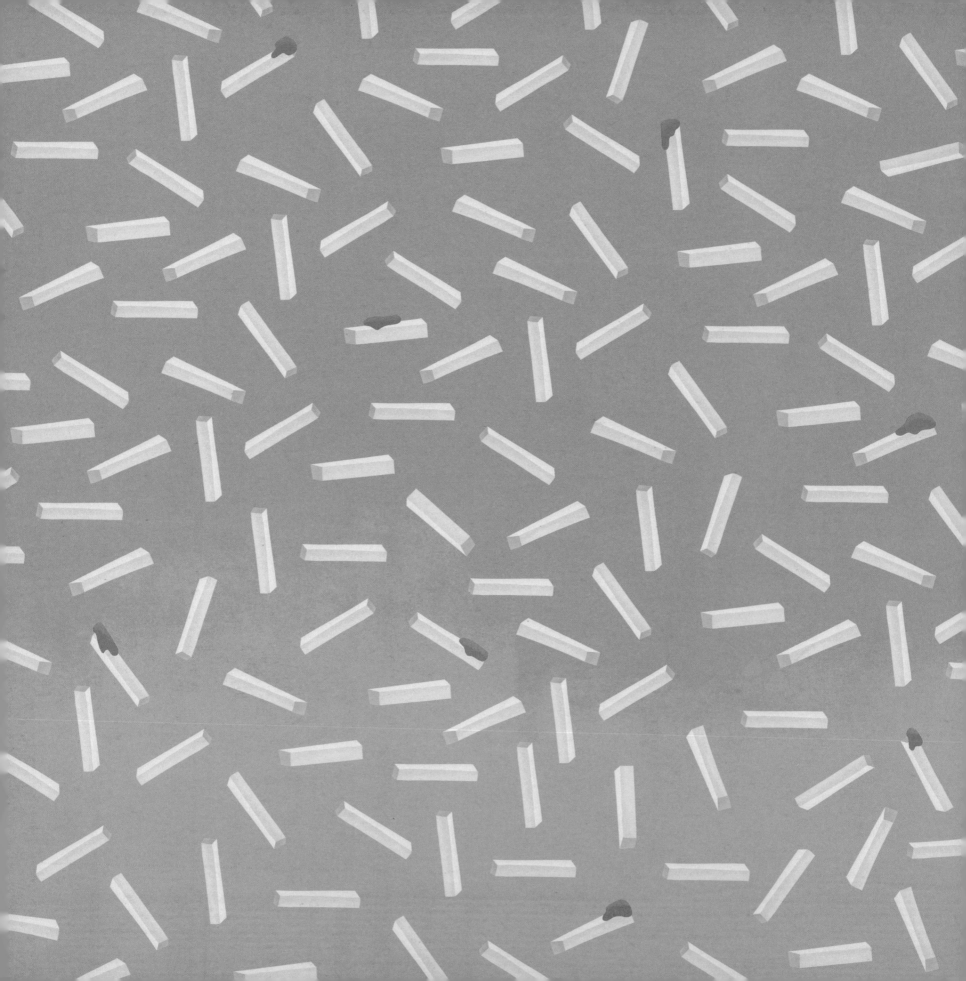